Fly Home, Blue!

by **Penny Dolan** and **Beccy Blake**

Blue the pigeon lived
in Grandad's tall shed.
But he was Tom's pigeon.
"Coo, coo, coo," went Blue
as he looked out of the shed,
waiting to fly.

3

4

Every day, Grandad let the pigeons

fly out of the shed.

They flew round and round together.

They looked like a big cloud.

Tom liked to see Blue fly up

into the sky.

One afternoon, Tom gave Blue
some seed.

He stroked Blue's feathers.

"Grandad says it will soon be time
for your first race," he said.

"You need to fly as fast as you can."

"Coo, coo, coo," went Blue.

Grandad and Tom took Blue
to a big lorry full of pigeons.
The birds stuck their beaks
out of the cages.
"Coo, coo, coo," they went.

Grandad helped to fasten the covers
and the lorry set off.

"Goodbye, Blue," called Tom, waving.

"See you tomorrow."

The lorry went on and on.

Night came and Blue went to sleep.

When he woke up, it was day again.

The lorry was in a big field.

Lots of people were waiting.

The pigeons were waiting too.

"Coo, coo, coo," went Blue as he got

ready to fly.

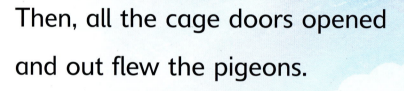

Then, all the cage doors opened
and out flew the pigeons.
Out flew Blue, up into the sky.
He looked around.
"That way," he thought.
"That way is home."

13

Blue flew over hills and rivers.

He flew over rocks and trees.

When it rained,

he stopped in a wood to keep dry.

When the sun came out,

he set off again.

15

At last, Blue saw sheds and flowers.
And Tom and Grandad were
there, calling Blue down.

Tom had seed for Blue to eat.

"I'm hungry," thought Blue,

and down he flew.

Blue landed on Tom's hand to get

the seed.

Grandad looked at his watch.

"That was fast. Well done, Blue,"

he said.

"Hooray for Blue!"

said Tom.

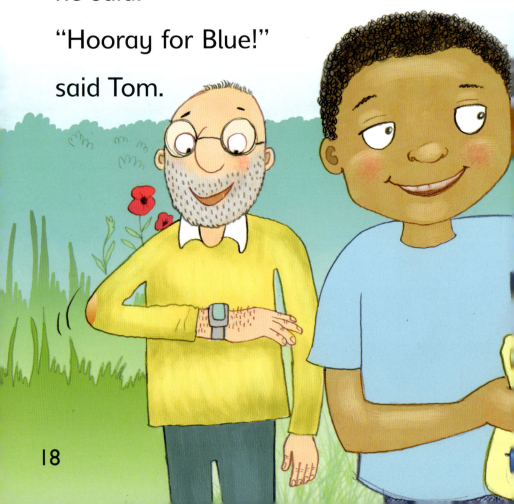

Blue was happy to be home again.

Story order

Look at these 5 pictures and captions.
Put the pictures in the right order
to retell the story.

1

The race begins.

2

Blue keeps dry during his race.

3

Tom and Grandad say goodbye to Blue.

4

Blue is happy to be home.

5

Tom feeds his pigeon, Blue.

Independent Reading

This series is designed to provide an opportunity for your child to read on their own. These notes are written for you to help your child choose a book and to read it independently.

In school, your child's teacher will often be using reading books which have been banded to support the process of learning to read. Use the book band colour your child is reading in school to help you make a good choice. *Fly Home, Blue!* is a good choice for children reading at Orange Band in their classroom to read independently.

The aim of independent reading is to read this book with ease, so that your child enjoys the story and relates it to their own experiences.

About the book

Blue the pigeon is about to fly in his first race. Tom and Grandad are excited to see whether Blue can find his way home, and how fast he can do it!

Before reading

Help your child to learn how to make good choices by asking:

"Why did you choose this book? Why do you think you will enjoy it?"

Look at the cover together and ask: "What do you think the story will be about?" Ask your child to think of what they already know about the story context. Then ask your child to read the title aloud. Establish that in this book, you will learn about racing pigeons.

Ask: "What do you know about pigeons? Are there any living in your neighbourhood?"

Remind your child that they can sound out the letters to make a word if they get stuck.

Decide together whether your child will read the story independently or read it aloud to you.

During reading

Remind your child of what they know and what they can do independently. If reading aloud, support your child if they hesitate or ask for help by telling the word. If reading to themselves, remind your child that they can come and ask for your help if stuck.

After reading

Support comprehension by asking your child to tell you about the story. Use the story order puzzle to encourage your child to retell the story in the right sequence, in their own words. The correct sequence can be found at the bottom of the next page.

Help your child think about the messages in the book that go beyond the story and ask: "Do you think the pigeons enjoy racing?" Give your child a chance to respond to the story: "Did you have a favourite part? Did you think Blue would make it home? Why/why not?"

Extending learning

Help your child understand the story structure by using the same sentence patterning and adding different elements. "Let's make up a new story about a fast animal. Which animal is your story about? What kind of race do they need to win? How can they use their speed and cleverness to be the winner?"

In the classroom, your child's teacher may be teaching how to use speech marks to show when characters are speaking.

There are many examples in this book that you could look at with your child. Find these together and point out how the end punctuation (comma, full stop or exclamation mark) comes inside the speech mark.

Franklin Watts
First published in Great Britain in 2020
by The Watts Publishing Group

Copyright © The Watts Publishing Group 2020

Series Editors: Jackie Hamley, Melanie Palmer and Grace Glendinning
Series Advisors: Dr Sue Bodman and Glen Franklin
Series Designer: Peter Scoulding

A CIP catalogue record for this book is
available from the British Library.

ISBN 978 1 4451 7091 6 (hbk)
ISBN 978 1 4451 7093 0 (pbk)
ISBN 978 1 4451 7092 3 (library ebook)

Printed in China

Franklin Watts
An imprint of
Hachette Children's Group
Part of The Watts Publishing Group
Carmelite House
50 Victoria Embankment
London EC4Y 0DZ

An Hachette UK Company
www.hachette.co.uk

www.franklinwatts.co.uk

Answer to Story order: 5, 3, 1, 2, 4